S0-AHN-796

JABBERWOCKY

Poem by

LEWIS CARROLL

Illustrated by

CHARLES SANTORE

RP | KIDS
PHILADELPHIA

Copyright © 2020 by Charles Santore
Cover copyright © 2020 by Hachette Book Group, Inc.

Hachette Book Group supports the right to free expression and the value of
copyright. The purpose of copyright is to encourage writers and artists to produce
the creative works that enrich our culture.

The scanning, uploading, and distribution of this book without permission
is a theft of the author's intellectual property. If you would like permission to use
material from the book (other than for review purposes), please contact
permissions@hbgusa.com. Thank you for your support of the author's rights.

Running Press Kids
Hachette Book Group
1290 Avenue of the Americas, New York, NY 10104
www.runningpress.com/rpkids
@RP_Kids

Printed in China

First Edition: August 2020

Published by Running Press Kids, an imprint of Perseus Books, LLC,
a subsidiary of Hachette Book Group, Inc. The Running Press Kids name and logo
is a trademark of the Hachette Book Group.

The Hachette Speakers Bureau provides a wide range of
authors for speaking events. To find out more, go to
www.hachettespeakersbureau.com or call (866) 376-6591.

The publisher is not responsible for websites (or their content)
that are not owned by the publisher.

Print book cover and interior design by Frances J. Soo Ping Chow.

Library of Congress Control Number: 2018959492

ISBNs: 978-0-7624-6543-9 (hardcover), 978-0-7624-6539-2 (ebook),
978-0-7624-6542-2 (ebook), 978-0-7624-6540-8 (ebook)

APS

10 9 8 7 6 5 4 3 2 1

TO

OLENKA

ILLUSTRATOR'S NOTE

After three challenging years illustrating *Alice's Adventures in Wonderland*, I decided to venture *Through The Looking Glass*. Once inside its world, I soon encountered "The Jabberwocky" and did not need to go farther; I knew that this was my next illustration project. The poem made me feel as if I were entering an ancient, arcane world where nothing ever changes. Yet, for a brief moment, this eternal, Arcadian landscape is disrupted by an incident—a blip—but everything subsequently continues on as it always has and always will.

The "blip" is, of course, a young man's quest to slay the fierce, monster-like Jabberwock. Fate has seemingly willed this quest and the young man readily accepts the challenge, slaying the fearsome beast in an epic battle. As the dust settles, life in this timeless place returns to normal, as though nothing ever happened. In visually creating this world, I owe a debt of gratitude to Martin Gardner's magnificent book *The Annotated Alice*. Reading it, I came to realize that "the words mean what they sound."

'Twas brillig, and the slithy toves
  Did gyre and gimble in the wabe:
All mimsy were the borogoves,
And the mome raths outgrabe.

"Beware the Jabberwock, my son!
The jaws that bite, the claws that catch!

Beware the Jubjub bird, and shun

The frumious
BANDERSNATCH!"

He took his vorpal sword in hand:
Long time the manxome foe he sought—

So rested he by the Tumtum tree,
And stood awhile in thought.

And, as in uffish thought he stood,
The Jabberwock, with eyes of flame,
Came whiffling through the tulgey wood,
And burbled as it came!

One, two! One, two! And through and through
The vorpal blade went snicker-snack!

He left it dead, and with its head
He went galumphing back.

"And hast thou slain the Jabberwock?
Come to my arms, my beamish boy!
O frabjous day! Callooh! Callay!"
He chortled in his joy.

'Twas brillig, and the slithy toves
Did gyre and gimble in the wabe:
All mimsy were the borogoves,
And the mome raths outgrabe.